For Jack
M·E·

For Bonnie
G·R·

First American edition published in 1996 by
Crocodile Books, USA
An imprint of Interlink Publishing Group, Inc.
99 Seventh Avenue, Brooklyn, New York 11215
Text © by Mark Ezra 1996
Illustrations © by Gavin Rowe 1996

Published simultaneously in Great Britain by Magi Publications.

Library of Congress Cataloging-in-Publication Data

Ezra, Mark
    The hungry otter / Mark Ezra ; pictures by Gavin Rowe. -- 1st
American ed.
        p.   cm.
    Summary: Because Little Otter helps save the life of a crow, he gets
help from this unexpected new friend when his own life is in danger.
    ISBN 1-56656-216-3
    [1. Otters--Fiction. 2. Crows--Fiction. 3. Friendship--Fiction.]
I. Rowe, Gavin, ill. II. Title.
PZ7.E987Hu 1996
[E]--dc20   96-8825
                                                              CIP
                                                              AC

Printed and bound in Belgium
10 9 8 7 6 5 4 3 2 1

MARK EZRA

The Hungry Otter

pictures by GAVIN ROWE

Crocodile Books, USA

An imprint of Interlink Publishing Group, Inc.
NEW YORK

Little Otter was feeling hungry.
"I'll go out to catch some fish," he said,
and before any of his brothers or sisters noticed
what he was doing, he launched himself out of his
bankside home and down into the water . . .

. . . but the water was not there!
Instead there was a glassy surface of solid ice.
Little Otter went slithering and skidding over it,
his paws scrabbling helplessly.

At last Little Otter was able to get to his feet.
He looked around and saw nothing but white
snow where the fields and green meadows
had once been. It all looked so strange
and unfamiliar.

Little Otter ran and jumped around in the snow for a while, and then he bounded off along the riverbank to find the mud slide where his family played each evening before sunset. He passed high frosted hedges and crossed a lane with deep frozen ruts.

Little Otter soon found the mud slide,
but it was set iron hard.
A large crow was already there, with his
feathers puffed out against the cold.

The crow flopped over on his back,
stuck his spindly legs in the air,
and scooted down the slide onto
the ice with a joyful croak.

The crow flapped his wings and took off into
the branches of a tree as the fox snapped at
his tail feathers.

Then the fox slipped and skidded down the
slide and across the ice.

Defeated, he picked himself up and loped off
angrily across the fields.

. . . the fox pounced.
Just at that moment, Little Otter
gave a cry of warning.

Little Otter was about to complain, "That's *my*
slide!" But then something caught his eye.
He saw a fox, silently creeping towards the crow.
The fox kept his body low and out of sight.
    The crow was so busy enjoying himself that
he didn't see the danger.
        Closer and closer the fox crawled,
until suddenly. . .

"Thank you," said the crow. "You saved my life.
But what are you doing here?"
"I came to find my mud slide," said Little Otter.
"And now I'm very hungry, because I can't catch
any fish. The river is all frozen over."
"That's easy to fix," said the crow. "Just leave
it to me."

The crow picked
up a large stone
in his beak,

flew high over the water, and dropped it.
With a loud CRACK it fell through the ice.

"There you are," said the crow. "Now you have a hole and can fish. Come to think of it, I'm pretty hungry, too, so while you're at it, catch one for me!"

Little Otter dove
into the water and
caught a fish for
the crow. . .

... but when he
went back to get
one for himself,
the fish were
watching. They
were not so easy
to catch.

Little Otter chased the fish downstream,
until at last he caught another one.
But when he tried to swim to the surface,
he could not find the hole!
Little Otter clawed at the ice, trying to
break through. He saw the blue sky above him,
but the thick ice lay between him and the fresh air.
Just as he thought he would drown in the freezing
water, he saw a black shape, high above him.

CRACK!
A heavy stone smashed through the ice,
making another hole.

Holding his fish, Little Otter scrambled out
of the river and lay on the bank, gasping for air.
The crow hopped over to him.
"One good turn deserves another," he said.
"You saved my life, and I saved yours!"

The crow flew back up to his perch to
finish off his fish, and Little Otter shook
his spiky fur dry.
Then, dragging his own fish behind him,
he made his way back home.